HERE'S HEATHCLIFF by Geo Gately

AMERICA'S CRAZIEST CAT!

Volume III

THE BEST OF SUNDAY WITH HEATHCLIFF

SPECIALTIES, ON THE HOUSE

TOR

A TOM DOHERTY ASSOCIATES BOOK

HEATHCLIFF: SPECIALTIES, ON THE HOUSE
Volume III of HERE'S HEATHCLIFF

Copyright © 1981 by McNaught Syndicate, Inc.

Reprinted by arrangement with Windmill Books, Inc. and Simon and Schuster, a division of Gulf and Western Corp.

A TOR Book

Published by Tom Doherty Associates
8-10 West 36 Street
New York, N.Y. 10018

First TOR printing: September 1985

ISBN: 0-812-56800-1
CAN. ED.: 0-812-56801-X

Printed in the United States of America

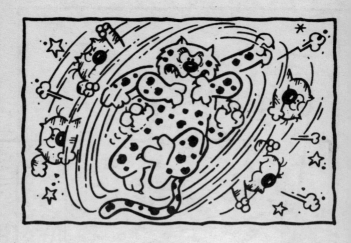

1977
McNaught Synd., Inc.

THE ART CRITIC

by Bob Gately

HI, RUTHIE!...I'M GLAD YOU STOPPED BY!....THERE'S SOMETHING I WANT TO SHOW YOU!

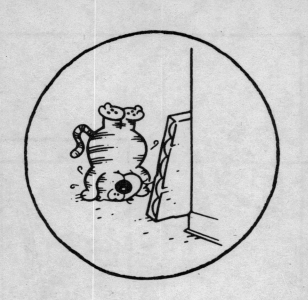

A METHOD TO HIS MADNESS

by Geo Gately

LOOK WHAT GRANDMA BOUGHT YOU!

THUMP-A-THUMP...

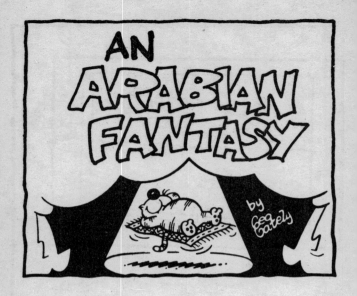

ADVENTURES OF A WATCHCAT

by Geo Gately

1977
McNaught
Syndicate, Inc.

THE TRANSFORMATION

HEY!... YOU CAN'T GO IN THERE!

4-17 1977
McNaught Synd., Inc.

THE SHUT-OUT

by geg Gately

6-5
1977
McNaught Synd., Inc.

HAVE YOU SEEN HEATHCLIFF, DEAR?

CHAMPIONSHIP FORM

by Geg Gately

HEATHCLIFF IS REALLY GREAT OFF THE HIGH BOARD!

THERE'S HEATHCLIFF, BUT HE WON'T COME IN UNLESS HE'S DRIVEN IN A CART LIKE A MAJOR LEAGUER!

DO YOU HAVE YOUR DOLL CARRIAGE OUT THERE? HOW 'BOUT USING THAT?

1977
6-26 McNaught Synd., Inc.

1977
McNaught Synd., Inc.